To Ryan,

you are awesome,
intelligent, and
extraordinary!

To Ryan,

you are awesome,
intelligent, and
extraordinary!

FRED and the MONSTER

A portion of proceeds from the sale of Fred and the Monster will be donated to First Book, a nonprofit organization that provides new books for children in need. Learn more about their work at www.firstbook.org

OCTOPUS INK
PRESS

Fred and the Monster
Text copyright © Scott Sussman 2014
Illustrations copyright © Yves Margarita 2014
All rights reserved.

ISBN 978-0-9829506-4-7
Library of Congress Control Number: 2014912198

Printed in China
The display type is set in Go Boom!

Visit our website at
www.octopusinkpress.com

FRED and the MONSTER

It was nighttime, and Fred was going to sleep.

"But Mom," he said, "can't I sleep with the lights on? Just once more?"

"You said that last night," said Fred's mom, "and the night before that. It's time you slept with the lights off like big boys do."

"But I'm afraid."

Placing a hand on Fred's shoulder, she said, "Inside of you there's a spark of courage. Find it. Then you'll see there's nothing to be afraid of."

Fred was silent as his mom kissed his forehead. She pulled up the sheets to his chin and turned off the light. As the door closed behind her, darkness surrounded him like a bat's wings.

Immediately, familiar sounds turned into frightening noises. Chirping crickets sounded like ghosts dragging chains. Croaking frogs became growling goblins.

As branches swayed and brushed against the window, Fred imagined monsters clawing the latch, ready to carry him away to the horrible lands they came from.

For more than an hour he tossed and turned, expecting gremlins to crawl through the electrical outlets.

Fred's eyelids had grown heavy when he heard the sound of teeth chattering. Someone—or something—was under his bed!

His heart started hammering. He was about to scream for his mom when a gruff voice spoke, freezing the words in his throat.

"C-c-could you p-please turn on a l-l-light?"

Fred's skin tingled as if a spider were crawling up his spine.

"P-p-please," the voice continued, "I'm af-f-f-f-fraid."

Biting his lower lip, Fred grabbed the flashlight from his bedside table. Slowly, he bent over the mattress and peeked under the bed.

There, hugging its tail to its chest, was the strangest creature. Shaped like a watermelon, it had carrot-colored skin and one eye in the center of its face. It had a thumb-sized horn on its head, and a single fang hanging from the corner of its mouth.

Fred screamed and fell out of bed. Striking the floor, he dropped the flashlight.

Terrified, he scrambled to retrieve the flashlight, but to his surprise when the beam shined in the monster's eye, the monster threw up its arms and rolled into a ball.

"Please don't hurt me!" it said, sobbing.

"You're afraid of me?" Fred asked.

Too frightened to look up, the monster nodded as tears streamed down its face.

"But you're a monster," Fred said. "You're not supposed to be afraid of anything."

The monster sniffed and wiped its eye.

"Here," Fred said, grabbing a tissue. But as he reached forward to hand the tissue to the monster, the monster scampered into a corner, trembling.

"What are you so scared of?"

"Everything," it said. "Especially the dark. Darkness is dangerous in my swamp." The monster looked up. "There are ferocious alligators, poisonous snakes, and stinging bees. Not to mention razor-sharp rocks and jagged stick bushes. And what if I got lost? Or fell off a cliff? The swamp is so cold and wet, but here under your bed I'm warm and safe. Best of all, there's always a light on. At least there was . . . Until tonight."

Remembering his mother's words, Fred said, "There's a spark of courage inside you. Find it. Then you won't be afraid."

"You think so?" the monster asked.

"I know so," Fred said, feeling calmer himself.

"Come on, I'll show you!"

Flashlight in hand, Fred climbed through the bedroom window as the monster followed, its tail dragging behind. They wandered down the street, turned the corner, and crossed the bridge.

As they entered the swamp, the monster clung to its tail like a security blanket. With its nerves in knots and its eye darting here and there, it shuddered at every shadow and jumped at every sound.

The night was cold and windy. Strange noises echoed in the darkness, while the sour stink of rotting vegetation filled the air.

While trudging over crushed weeds and wild grass, suddenly Fred heard a gasp and the sound of feet shuffling over damp leaves. Twirling around and directing the flashlight, he saw the monster staring with its eye wide open, pointing at a twisted shadow that looked like a giant open-mouthed alligator.

But when Fred shined the flashlight at the massive shape, all he saw was a gnarled tree.

Fred and the monster continued through the swamp, stepping over roots and stooping under branches. While Fred was parting some dangling vines, the monster screamed.

Fred's heart leaped into his throat. He aimed the light at the monster's foot. Lying in a clump on the ground was a vine, which the monster had mistaken for a snake.

The air was sticky wet as they slogged through clouds of mist and throngs of thorn-riddled bushes. While maneuvering through an area of jutting twigs and crooked sticks, Fred heard an angry buzzing.

Before he could flinch, a sound like a cracking whip echoed in his ear as a blast of air brushed his neck. Fred spun around.

There was the monster holding its tail and grinning. It had whacked a fist-sized bee that now struggled to escape from a puddle of slime.

The monster lifted its chin and smiled, its one eye twinkling with pride.

"Way to go!" Fred said, high-fiving the monster.

After tiptoeing around a mucky pond, they slipped between two moss-covered boulders and arrived at the monster's lair.

The monster yawned, and then extended a furry paw for Fred to shake.

"Thanks, friend! You were right. I just had to find a little courage."

The monster plopped down into a pile of leaves, curled into a ball, and fell fast asleep.

Fred switched off the flashlight and laid it near the monster's head . . . just in case.

Then he walked home by moonlight.

Back in his room, Fred removed his muddy sneakers and slipped into bed.

He wanted to turn on the light but, remembering the spark of courage inside him, he decided not to.

Before falling asleep, however, he pulled out his spare flashlight and set it on the bedside table . . . just in case.

Also from
OCTOPUS INK PRESS

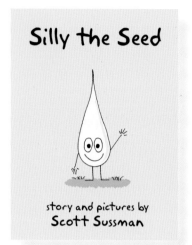

Silly the Seed

Silly the Seed is the heroic adventure of a small seed that grows up to be a beautiful flower. Along the way his acts of friendship and kindness teach and entertain readers of all ages. But when Silly needs help, who will help him?

Weird the Beard

Weird the Beard is the amusing journey of a beard that makes friends by cracking jokes. But the joke's on Weird when he tries to befriend a suspicious-looking razor. Needless to say, he will never be the same.

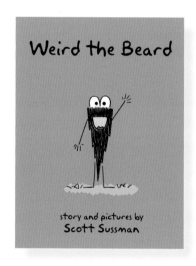

Lerky the Handturkey

Lerky the Handturkey is the inspiring story of a handturkey whose wise words encourage others to see the bright side. It's the companion to Silly the Seed and Weird the Beard, a wacky tale of friendship and optimism.

Also from
OCTOPUS INK PRESS

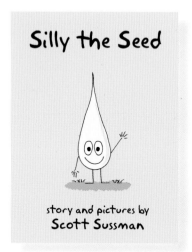

Silly the Seed

Silly the Seed is the heroic adventure of a small seed that grows up to be a beautiful flower. Along the way his acts of friendship and kindness teach and entertain readers of all ages. But when Silly needs help, who will help him?

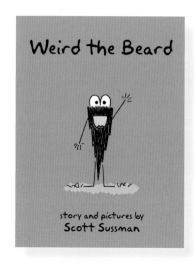

Weird the Beard

Weird the Beard is the amusing journey of a beard that makes friends by cracking jokes. But the joke's on Weird when he tries to befriend a suspicious-looking razor. Needless to say, he will never be the same.

Lerky the Handturkey

Lerky the Handturkey is the inspiring story of a handturkey whose wise words encourage others to see the bright side. It's the companion to Silly the Seed and Weird the Beard, a wacky tale of friendship and optimism.

Mark and the Molecule Maker

When Mark enters his father's laboratory and finds the Molecule Maker, he flips the switch and makes a monster. Things go from bad to worse when the creature escapes and Mark races against the sunrise to right the wrong.

Mark and the Molecule Maker 2: The Lightning Jungle

The adventure continues with book two of the Mark and the Molecule Maker Trilogy. When the Molecule Maker malfunctions, creating a horde of mischievous creatures that kidnap Mark's father, Mark charges into the lightning jungle on an amazing rescue mission. But will he arrive before it's too late?

Mark and the Molecule Maker 3: The Underground Mountain

In the thrilling conclusion to the Mark and the Molecule Maker Trilogy, the chase is on when a cunning monster steals the Molecule Maker. In a desperate attempt to retrieve the extraordinary invention, Mark and his father must risk their lives on the treacherous underground mountain, where danger lurks behind every boulder and hides inside every hole.

Visit our website at www.octopusinkpress.com
for updates and information regarding future publications.